KAREN WALLACE'S
Spooky Beasts

Two grippingly ghostly stories!

Illustrated by Judy Brown

Also by Karen Wallace in Happy Cat Books

Fearless Fiona

The Mystery of the Great Stone Haggis

The Mothproof Hall Mystery

Published by
Happy Cat Books
An imprint of Catnip Publishing Ltd
Islington Business Centre
3-5 Islington High Street
London N1 9LQ

This edition first published 2007
1 3 5 7 9 10 8 6 4 2

Copyright © Karen Wallace, 1995
Illustrations © Judy Brown, 1995
The moral rights of the author/ illustrator have been asserted

A CIP catalogue record for this book is available from
the British Library

ISBN: 978-1-905117-46-8
Printed in Poland

www.catnippublishing.co.uk

Contents

Thunder and Lightning

Chapter One

Once there were two old ladies called
Violet Sniff and Enid Greenfly. They
lived together at 31 Oak Tree Terrace.

Violet Sniff and Enid Greenfly had
lived together for over forty years and
everything they did, they did together.

They complained about their neighbours
together. They wrote nasty letters about
other people's untidy gardens together.
They even shook their heads and clicked
their tongues together when they saw
children riding their bicycles or playing
in the lane or even *looking* as if they were
having a good time.

Violet Sniff and Enid Greenfly were definitely not the kind of old ladies you would like to share a desert island with, or even a three-minute bus ride, for that matter.

One day in late October (it was almost Hallowe'en) Violet Sniff and Enid Greenfly were working in their garden. Violet was cleaning up leaves with a hoover. The garden was almost entirely paved in concrete slabs so a hoover was the best tool for the job. Enid was polishing the gnome that had stood patiently fishing in the blue plastic pond for as long as anyone could remember.

"Messy little brutes," muttered Violet as she pushed the hoover over some leaves that had fallen from an old oak tree.

The sound of muffled giggling from next door came through the hedge.

"I blame their parents," snapped Enid and she gave the gnome such a hard rub, it almost removed his left ear.

Violet Sniff glared at the oak leaves with eyes that looked like stewed plums.

"I wouldn't mind if it was a monkey puzzle tree," she said in a bad-tempered voice. "They've got nice sharp, spikey leaves that don't fall off."

"It's the children *playing* inside it, that I can't stand," snarled Enid. "In my book, if a tree is hollow, it should be chopped down!" Whap! The gnome got a nasty flick on the back of his neck with her polishing cloth.

"Talking about books," said Violet, her bony hand tightening around the hoover handle. "How many times have we complained about this tree?"

Enid put down her polishing cloth and pulled out a thick black book from her pocket. It looked like an address book with the alphabet down the edge of the pages. Inside was a record of all the complaints she and Violet had ever made.

She ran her finger down to T for Tree and flipped open the page. "Seventy-three," she said triumphantly. "And that doesn't include the ones about Noise, Children, Inconvenience and Leaves."

At that moment there was a shout of laughter and a bright orange ball sailed over the hedge. It bounced once, rolled across the concrete slabs and stopped at the gnome's feet.

Two children's faces appeared above the lowest branch of the oak tree. They were Sally and Heather Hughes and they lived next door. Sally and Heather were nice little girls who had been brought up to always be polite to old ladies.

"I'm terribly sorry," said Heather. "May we please…"

"No, you can't," snarled Enid Greenfly. "It's mine now." She grabbed the ball in her lumpy purple hands and jabbed it with the pair of scissors she wore on a string around her waist.

Sally opened her mouth to speak.

"Get lost!" yelled Violet Sniff. And she kicked the ruined ball across the garden where it hit the old oak tree with a resounding *thump*.

The two faces disappeared.

Inside the hollow tree, a small round bottle hidden there almost four hundred years before, wobbled in its hiding place. Then it fell to the ground and rolled out on to the concrete.

"Now what?" muttered Violet Sniff.
She bent down and picked the bottle
up. It was made out of blue glass with
a glass stopper stuck firmly in its neck.
DO NOT OPEN was written in spidery
letters across the front.

Violet tipped the strange bottle upside
down. There didn't seem to be anything
inside it. "What do you think this is?" she
said to Enid Greenfly.

"Litter," snapped Enid Greenfly.

Violet Sniff read the spidery writing
again.

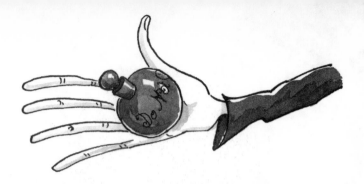

"Huh," she said. "Nobody tells me what to do." And she threw the bottle into a big metal dustbin where it smashed into a hundred pieces.

Chapter Two

That night the moon hung in the sky
like a big yellow plate. It shone down on
the gnome still patiently fishing by the
blue plastic pond. And it shone on the
big metal dustbin that stood by the back
door. At the bottom of the dustbin lay
the bits of blue bottle.

No one but the gnome saw a thin plume of smoke curl up from the dustbin and into the cold night air. No one but the gnome saw the smoke coil like a snake over the concrete slabs towards the pond. It was an odd-looking snake with two bumps on its back and as the gnome watched, the bumps pulled apart and turned into two extraordinary-looking cats.

The gnome had seen a lot of cats in his time but he had never seen cats like these two. They had fur that shone like silver. They had sharp white teeth that flashed in the moonlight. But the most peculiar thing of all was the colour of their eyes. One cat had purple eyes and the other had red ones.

It takes a lot to make a gnome speak. In fact, when the gnome thought about it later, he had never spoken at all before that night. But now, as he stared at the glittering eyes and the sharp teeth, he suddenly couldn't help himself. "Who are you?" he gasped.

"I'm Thunder," said the cat with purple eyes.

"I'm Lightning," said the one with red eyes. "We're witches' cats."

"Where have you come from?" asked the gnome.

Thunder grinned. "From inside a bottle," he said. "Some Nasty Old Bag put a spell on us and bottled us up for four hundred years."

"People did things like that four hundred years ago," explained Lightning.

"Hold on," said the gnome suspiciously. "I thought witches' cats were supposed to be black."

"We are," said Lightning. "At least, when we have our own witches, we are."

"When's Hallowe'en?" asked Thunder suddenly.

The gnome looked puzzled. "Tomorrow night," he said. "Why?"

Thunder's purple eyes blazed. "It's our last chance to find new witches," he said.

"Does that mean you'll turn black?" asked the gnome who was beginning to wonder if he was going mad after all those years of not talking.

"Once they become our very *own* witches, we will," said Lightning. He rubbed his head against the gnome's green boot. Sparks fizzed in the night. "You haven't seen any witches around here, have you?" he purred, coaxingly.

"We'll grant you a wish if you help us," said Thunder in a silvery voice.

"Look here," said the gnome, going hot under his painted red jacket with the silly buttons down the front. "This talk about witches is all very well but times have changed. You don't get witches anymore.

Lightning leapt on to the gnome's shoulder. "How do you know?" he whispered. "Who lives in this house, for instance?"

"Violet Sniff and Enid Greenfly,"
said the gnome stiffly. "But they're not
witches."

As he spoke he remembered the *whap*
of the duster on the back of his neck. "At
least, not your kind of witches."

"Are you *sure*?" asked Lightning his red
eyes glowing like coals.

"They might be," purred Thunder.

"Huh," said the gnome. "And I might catch a fish."

The two cats looked at each other and grinned. Something like a bolt of blue light passed between them.

Suddenly the gnome felt an unmistakable tug. He knew at once it was the tug he had been hoping to feel for as long as he could remember.

With his plaster heart thumping like a sledgehammer, he jerked his rod into the air, and there it was – a big golden fish dangling on the end of his line!

"Galloping Garden Centres!" cried the gnome.

He spun round to look for the strange silver cats. But Thunder and Lightning had disappeared.

Chapter Three

The next morning Enid Greenfly came
downstairs to the kitchen early. It was
the Pillars of Society meeting in the
Town Hall that day. Geranium Booby,
Mayoress, President and Bossiest Women
in the Universe was going to be there.

Both Enid and Violet were VIPs or Very Important Pillars. And that morning, there were lots of things they planned to force other people to do.

"Breakfast!" called Enid, dolloping marmite into two bowls of branflakes and filling them up to the top with warm water.

Upstairs, Violet Sniff wound her grey hair into a bun and fixed it with a hair pin as long as a knitting needle. Then she belted herself into a black dress that had VIP embroidered in red letters across the front. "That'll show 'em," she muttered.

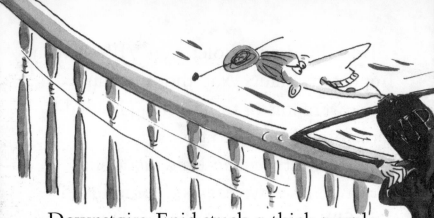

Downstairs, Enid stuck a thick purple finger into Violet's bowl of branflakes. "Hurry up," she yelled. "It's getting cold."

Violet Sniff turned to walk down the stairs. Then suddenly she did something she had never done before. Something she had never even thought of doing before. Violet Sniff hitched up her sensible black dress and slid down the banisters straight into the kitchen.

"Violet!" cried Enid. "What on *earth* do you think you're doing?"

Violet Sniff stared open-mouthed at Enid Greenfly. "Me?" she spluttered. "What on earth do you think *you're* doing?"

Enid Greenfly had a black dustbin bag tied to her shoulders and was riding around the kitchen on a floor polisher!

"Miiaow!" cried a voice.

"Miiaow!" cried another.

Two little cats sat looking like Christmas decorations on the kitchen counter.

Violet and Enid stared at them.

Now Violet knew that as far as Enid was concerned the best place for a cat was at the bottom of a swamp attached to a lump of concrete. And Enid knew that Violet felt the same about cats as she felt about children, which is to say, they should not be seen or heard or indeed be taken any notice of whatsoever.

Neither Enid Greenfly nor Violet Sniff spoke a word. All you could hear was the sound of the kitchen clock ticktocking on the wall.

Thunder gazed at Violet with his strange purple eyes. Lightning jumped down and rubbed his shiny silver body against Enid's ankles.

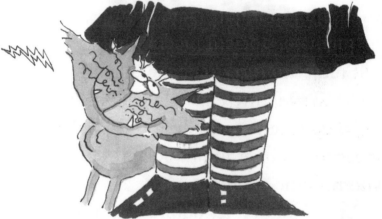

"Aren't they *adorable*?" cried Enid. And she stepped off the floor polisher and gathered up Lightning in her arms.

"What *boootiful* purple eyes!" cooed Violet, burying her bony nose in Thunder's furry stomach.

The two cats looked at each other. Something like a bolt of blue light passed between them.

"Enid," said Violet Sniff suddenly. "When's Hallowe'en?"

"Hallowe'en is tonight," said Enid Greenfly and her lumpy face began to twitch in the strangest way.

"Enid," said Violet again. "I'm not going to the Pillars of Society meeting this morning."

"That's funny," said Enid. "Nor am I."

As she spoke, her eyes travelled across the kitchen to where two brooms were standing in a corner. One was yellow

with blue bristles and the other was
green with orange bristles.

Without speaking, Violet took the
yellow one and Enid grabbed the green
one.

"I fancy some dried toad for supper,"
said Violet climbing on to her broom as
if it was the most natural thing in the
world to do. Then she pulled the knitting
needle out of her bun and a tangle of
grey hair fell over her shoulders.

"What about some tinned lizard to go
with the dried toad?" said Enid Greenfly,
climbing on to her own broom. "By the

way," she added almost shyly. "I like your hair."

Violet Sniff grinned like an old alligator. "I was just thinking of

dying bits of it orange," she said. "For
Hallowe'en."

"Hallowe'en! Hallowe'en!" cried Enid
Greenfly, cantering out of the kitchen on
the back of her broomstick. "We have to
get a pumpkin!"

"What about our pussycats?" cried
Violet Sniff. "We can't go without
them!" "They can come with us," said
Enid Greenfly. "They can ride on our
shoulders!"

"I think we've found our witches," said Thunder to Lightning as they were carried at full gallop out of the front door. "What colour's my tail?"

"Black!" cried Lightning from behind. He twisted his head round. "So's mine!"

"It's working!" cried Thunder.

Chapter Four

"Look here, Miss Sniff," said Mr Wrench the dentist. "Are you sure about this? I won't be able to put them back, you know."

"If three's good enough for Enid, then three's good enough for me," said Violet Sniff firmly. As she spoke the black and white cat that sat on her shoulder, purred loudly and rubbed his face against her ear. It was almost as if he was whispering something to her.

From the corner of the room, Enid Greenfly grinned a huge grin. She had one tooth on the top and two teeth on the bottom. "We don't *want* them back," she said, kissing her own black and white cat. "And the funny thing was, pulling them out didn't hurt one little bit."

Mr Wrench shuddered. Not only were Violet and Enid founder members of the Pillars of Society, they were Very Important Pillars, just like he was. Only last week they had proposed that Hallowe'en should be abolished and that children should visit the dentist every Saturday.

Now, here was Enid Greenfly dressed up in a grubby black mackintosh having her teeth pulled out, and as for Violet Sniff—she was wearing a torn black skirt and her hair looked like a bird's nest with orange peel stuck in it.

Something very peculiar was going on.

"Stop staring and get on with it," snapped Violet Sniff, prodding him with a bony finger. "We're in a hurry. It's almost Hallowe'en."

Mr Wrench shuddered again.

Five minutes later, with six teeth between them, Violet Sniff and Enid Greenfly were laughing their heads off and cantering down the corridor on their brooms. It was a funny sounding noise, thought Mr Wrench. More like a cackle than a laugh. He took a deep breath, then he picked up the telephone and rang the Town Hall.

"Get me Geranium Booby," he said. "It's Digby Wrench here."

"I'm sorry, the Mayoress is in an emergency Pillars of Society meeting right now," said a voice.

"Well, get her out of it," said Mr Wrench. "This is an emergency, too."

There was a click on the line.

"What do you want?" squawked a voice like a field full of crows.

"Geranium," said Digby Wrench. "I've just seen Violet Sniff and Enid Greenfly. We've got to do something."

"What do you think we're having a meeting about?" shouted Geranium Booby. "One of the Pillars saw them in the supermarket this morning demanding half a pound of dried toads and a cauldron." She paused. "And another saw one of them carrying a pumpkin on her head and—"

She stopped as if what she was about to say was just too horrible.

"What else were they doing?" demanded Digby.

"They were eating ice-creams on the street," spluttered Geranium Booby at last. "I just don't know what's got into them."

"There's certainly something very strange about their new pets," said Digby Wrench cautiously.

"What pets?" asked Geranium Booby. "They hate animals."

"The black and white cats," said Digby Wrench.

"What black and white cats?" asked Geranium Booby.

"The ones that sit on their shoulders and whisper in their ears," blurted Digby Wrench. "I tell you Geranium, there's something peculiar going on."

There was a long silence.

"Digby," said Geranium Booby slowly. "Does one cat have purple eyes and the other have red ones?" Suddenly, she sounded hollow and ghostly as if she was whispering in a cave.

On the other end of the line, Digby Wrench felt a cold wind blowing out of the telephone. "How did you know?" he gasped.

But Geranium Booby appeared not to hear him. "There's no time to lose," she said in a low eerie voice. "Meet me at Oak Tree Terrace." Then the line went dead.

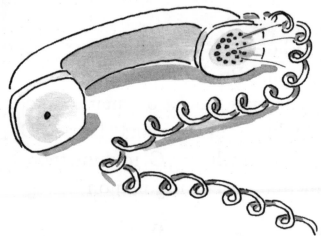

"Rampaging Rosebushes!" muttered the gnome. It was the first time he had seen Violet Sniff and Enid Greenfly since the blue bottle had smashed in the dustbin. The gnome blinked and looked again.

Two witchy-looking old ladies were cackling with laughter as they dragged a large iron cauldron across the concrete slabs. On their shoulders sat two black cats, at least they were almost black—

there was still a tiny patch of white in the middle of their foreheads.

"Ahem!" said the gnome in a rather embarrassed way.

Lightning gazed at him with glowing red eyes. "Yes?"

"Are you the white witches' cats I met last night?"

"We are," said Thunder.

The gnome wiped a gloved hand over

his bushy eyebrows. "Violet Sniff and Enid Greenfly," he began. "Are they, um, witches, now? That is, are they, um, *your* witches?"

Thunder nodded and rubbed his nose against Violet's ear. She smelt of bonfires and sweetpapers. "I'm rather fond of mine," he said.

Lightning grinned and sank his claws into Enid's shoulder. "Nice pussycat," she murmured and stroked his neck.

"It really is most extraordinary," said Violet Sniff, as she and Enid heaved the cauldron on to a smouldering bonfire. "I do believe this is the first time in my life I've ever felt really happy."

Violet shook her tangled grey hair and laughed. "How could we have belonged to the Very Important Pillars Society?" she said. "They're so bossy and mean and are always telling people what to do."

"And as for that Geranium Booby," said Enid.

"I never really liked her," said Violet.

"I've always been a bit afraid of her," said Enid.

Violet grinned her almost toothless grin. "She's nothing but a Nasty Old Bag," she said firmly.

As she spoke the hairs on the back of Thunder's neck began to prickle. Suddenly he sensed danger. It was a Nasty Old Bag who had locked them in a bottle four hundred years ago, and even though four hundred years is a long time, once a Nasty Old Bag, always a Nasty Old Bag.

Thunder looked across at Lightning. "I've got a funny feeling about this Nasty Old Bag," he hissed. "We might have to make a quick getaway."

Lightning nodded and stared at the two coloured brooms that Violet and Enid had left on the ground. "But first we have to test those brooms," he muttered. "I've never flown a *plastic* one before."

"We have to make our witches try them out," said Thunder.

"How?" asked Lightning.

"I'll make the pumpkin disappear," said Lightning. "Then they'll have to get another one."

He closed his eyes. There was a bolt of blue light and the huge pumpkin that was sitting by the bonfire disappeared into thin air.

Violet bent over the cauldron and sniffed the bubbling grey liquid they had prepared. It was their first proper witches' brew and they wanted to get it right. "Delicious," she murmured. "A bit more toad, perhaps?"

Enid dipped in a thick purple finger and licked it, then she picked up a tattered-looking cookbook. "Now add your pumpkin," she read aloud.

"Violet!" shrieked Enid Greenfly. "The pumpkin's gone and it's almost Hallowe'en! We'll never find another one in time!"

"Don't worry dear," said Violet Sniff in a matter-of-fact voice. "We're witches now. We'll fly to the supermarket and buy one."

"Of course we will," said Enid, wiping away her tears. "How silly of me."

They picked up their brooms and climbed on.

"Let's think *witch*," said Violet firmly.

Enid squeezed her eyes shut and thought *witch* as hard as she could.

Slowly, very slowly, Violet Sniff and
Enid Greenfly rose off the ground. They
rose above the bonfire. They rose above
the hedge. Then there was a *phut* and
clunk and they sank down beside the blue
plastic pond.

"Honestly," said the gnome looking at
Thunder and Lightning with his clever
blue eyes. "You should know plastic
brooms don't fly."

Suddenly a voice like a field full of
crows ripped through the
night.

"Violet! Enid!" screeched Geranium Booby. "We're all here. All the VIPs! Don't move! We know what's best for you!"

Thunder's fur stood on end. "It's her," he hissed. "It's the Nasty Old Bag who locked us up."

Behind them there was a sound of splintering wood as the back door was kicked to the ground.

"Quick!" shouted the gnome. "Take these!" In his hands were two brooms—the old fashioned kind you can buy at garden centres. They were made of wood with sticks tied to the end and they looked just like witches' brooms.

Violet Sniff and Enid Greenfly stared at the brooms but they were unable to move or think. The sound of Geranium Bobby's voice had frozen them like statues.

The trampling of sensible shoes grew nearer…

There was no time to lose! Thunder and Lightning locked eyes and a bolt of blue light exploded into the night. A split second later Violet and Enid grabbed the wooden brooms and jumped on to them.

"You won't get away this time," snarled Geranium Bobby, glaring at Thunder and Lightning with a look of pure poison. But as she spoke, Thunder and Lightning became completely black, and their eyes turned the deepest purple and the brightest red.

"Oh yes, we will!" cried Violet Sniff and Enid Greenfly letting out an earsplitting cackle. And the wooden brooms roared into the air, high over the top of the old oak tree.

"Make a wish! A witch's first wish!" cried Thunder and Lightning.

"What shall it be?" cried their very own witches.

"Something you really want!" cried Thunder and Lightning.

Violet Sniff looked down at Geranium Booby, shaking her fist in the air. She was the bossiest woman in the Universe. She was a Nasty Old Bag. Violet felt as if she had been under Geranium Booby's spell for years and years so she closed her eyes and made her first witch's wish.

A horrible yowl floated up from the ground. *SPLOT!* Geranium Booby fell backwards into the pond, her legs and arms waggling about like a monstrous spider.

Violet Sniff hooted with laughter and
then she heard the most extraordinary
noise. All the other VIPs were laughing
too. It was as if a tremendous spell had
finally been broken.

Meanwhile Enid Greenfly swooped over the house next door where Sally and Heather Hughes lived and made *her* first witch's wish.

From out of the top of the oak tree a brand new orange ball bounced on to Sally and Heather's garden, rolled slowly across the grass and stopped outside their back door.

"We did it!" cried Thunder.

"We're free!" cried Lightning.

"We're witches!" cried Violet Sniff and Enid Greenfly. "Yippee!"

Thunder looked at Lightning then both of them looked down. Something like a bolt of blue light passed between them and far below, beside the plastic pond, the gnome felt *another* unmistakable tug on his line! He couldn't believe his luck.

"Colliding Compost Containers!" cried the gnome as the rod jumped in his hand. "This one feels like a whale!"

Snapper Bites Back

Chapter One

Clever Trevor yawned and climbed
down from his high chair beside the
swimming pool. It was a hard life being
a lifeguard. All day he had to flex his
muscles and look tough. Then he had to
get down from his chair and walk round
and round the edge of the pool. It was
a rolling, bow-legged walk, a bit like a
cowboy who has been sitting on a saddle
all week. It was how all tough lifeguards

were supposed to walk and it had taken him a long time to learn.

Clever Trevor sighed. The truth was it didn't matter what he did. Nobody seemed to notice how tough and handsome he really was. Nobody, that is, except his friend Bulging Brian.

Bulging Brian was also a lifeguard. He was tough and handsome and he had forearms like joints of boiling bacon. He also had a head the size of a hard-boiled egg. Bulging Brian was about as smart as a hard-boiled egg, too.

"Saved anyone recently?" asked Bulging Brian as the two of them were changing after a long, hard day by the pool.

"Nah," said Clever Trevor. "Too busy."

Bulging Brian nodded knowingly. "By the time you've decided which dive to do—"

"Yeah," said Clever Trevor. "It's usually too late."

"Yeah," agreed Bulging Brian as he pulled on his tight leopard-skin trousers and his 'Hunks Have It All' sweat-shirt. "Got any plans for this evening?"

Clever Trevor looked in the mirror. He was deeply tanned as if he had just come back from holiday. The tube of Top to Toe Tan Treatment had said: Use as needed.

Clever Trevor smirked to himself. He had needed the whole lot.

"Same as usual," he replied.

Bulging Brian grinned. "You mean, go home. Get dressed. Go out and show off."

"Yeah."

Clever Trevor and Bulging Brian pushed through the revolving doors on to the street. Neither of them noticed the little old lady who went flying out the other side.

"See ya at the club then," said Bulging Brian as he slicked back his gluey blonde hair.

Clever Trevor climbed into his buttercup-yellow sports car and revved the engine so loudly, a baby in a pushchair began to howl. Then he roared off down the street, shaking leaves from the trees and frightening little old ladies as they pruned roses in their front gardens.

There was a pile of letters waiting when he got home. Actually, they were mostly brochures and special offers. Clever Trevor filled out all the coupons he could find because he liked to have lots of envelopes to open. It made him feel popular. Sometimes, if the envelopes were easy to open, he would stick them down again so that if he didn't get a lot of letters the next day, he could always open the old ones again.

At any rate, it wasn't often that he got a proper letter so Clever Trevor was surprised to find himself looking at a plain white envelope with his name typewritten on the front. Not only that, the name on the front was his real name, Trevor Prat, which was a

secret to be kept from as many people
as possible.

Clever Trevor read the letter. Then he
read it again. Then he made himself a
cup of tea with five teaspoons of sugar
and half a tin of evaporated milk. Then
he sat down and read the letter again.

His Great Aunt Emily had died and
left him Molehills, the farm she had lived
in all her life.

At first Clever Trevor was astounded.
He had never known his aunt very well.
But after a while, he began to get used
to the idea. In fact, he rather fancied
owning lots of land and not doing
much.

"So you're going to be a farmer," said Bulging Brian as the two of them sat at the bar of *Nerds*, their favourite nightclub. "Um, what exactly does a farmer do?"

Clever Trevor sucked at something red and fizzy through a long straw. "They drink tea and watch television, mostly," he said. He blew a few bubbles and stared into his glass in a moody, movie-star way. "And sometimes, in the middle of the night, they have to get up and, ah, milk the chickens."

"Wow," said Bulging Brian, looking at his friend in a completely new light. "That's amazing."

Chapter Two

As the buttercup-yellow sports car lurched down the muddy track to Molehills Farm, Clever Trevor tried to recall what he remembered about his Great Aunt Emily.

All he could think of was a bristly little woman, who sucked a pipe and always wore trousers and had a terrier called Snapper who never left her side. Once, when Clever Trevor was six, Great Aunt Emily had sent him a toy farm with real hay and bits of wood cut up into tiny logs. But he hadn't like the smell so his mother had taken it away and given him a Batman costume instead.

The sports car plunged into a deep puddle, spraying mud all over the windscreen. Clever Trevor flicked on the wipers. Suddenly he was in the middle of a farmyard, staring at a large brick house with the words Molehills Farm written in black letters on top of the front gate.

Clever Trevor got out of the car, strolled towards the house with his rolling cowboy walk, slipped and fell flat on his face in the greasy mud that covered the yard. There was a snort of laughter behind him.

"I'm terribly sorry," said a girl wearing gumboots and a muddy overall. "I didn't mean to laugh. You just looked so funny."

Clever Trevor glared at her. He wasn't supposed to look funny. He was supposed to look tough and handsome.

"Who are you?" he asked rudely as he clambered to his feet.

"I'm Nellie Bucket," said the girl. "I've been looking after your aunt's farm." She paused. "I've been expecting you."

Clever Trevor stared at her. She wore glasses and a bobble hat and didn't seem to have any lipstick on. He had never seen a girl wearing a bobble hat before. And he had never spoken to one who didn't wear lipstick.

"Well, you don't have to bother any more," he said, wiping the mud out of his eyes. "I know all about farming."

Nellie Bucket gave him a strange look. "But I thought you were a—" She blushed. "There's just the milking to do," she said quickly, and she put down the pitchfork she had been carrying and walked away across the yard.

Clever Trevor looked beyond her to a group of chickens in the orchard. They were pecking grass and seemed perfectly happy. They didn't look as if they needed milking.

He walked up the path and opened the front door.

A picture of Great Aunt Emily was hanging in front of him. In one hand she held her terrier, Snapper. The other hand rested on a long knobbly stick.

Clever Trevor looked at his great aunt's face. Then he looked at the terrier. The two of them were almost identical, except that his aunt looked a bit fiercer.

A fire was burning in the sitting room and a pot of tea and biscuits had been laid out on a table in front of the television. That's more like it, thought Clever Trevor, not stopping to wonder who had done it for him.

He gazed around the room. There were pictures on the wall, the sofa and chairs looked comfortable and in front of the fire was a handmade rug with a picture of a terrier woven into the middle. Above the fire...Ugh!

What on earth is that? thought Clever Trevor, and he leant forward to get a better look. There must be some mistake, he thought. That bossy girl must have put it there as a joke.

Above the fire, in pride of place, was a battered metal dish with a name engraved on it.

Ugh! Ugh! It was a dog bowl!

Clever Trevor puffed himself up to his full height and even though no one was watching, he stuck out his square jaw and looked tough.

"I'm not having a dog bowl in my sitting room," he muttered. He opened the window, threw out the bowl and watched as it skidded across the yard and landed underneath a rosebush.

Grrrr!

It was a low, menacing sound.

Grrrr! Grrrr!

Clever Trevor spun round. It sounded just like…

Brrrrrmmm! Brrrrrmmm! There was a squeal of tyres in the yard and mud splattered all over the window. Bulging Brian jumped off his bike and shambled across the yard.

"Watch out for the—" yelled Clever Trevor, but he was too late.

Bugling Brian skidded on the mud and slid on his nose right up to the gate.

As Clever Trevor turned to leave the room, he looked up at the bare wall where the dog bowl had been. It would be a good place to hang that big picture of himself in his pink and green swimming trunks with all his life-saving medals hung round his neck.

"Funny that noise, though." Clever Trevor shrugged. Must have been the central heating pipes, he thought, wisely. Old pipes make all sorts of strange sounds. He'd heard about it on a video somewhere. But as Clever Trevor walked down the hall to open the front door, a peculiar thought occurred to him: he hadn't seen any radiators in the house.

Chapter Three

That night Clever Trevor slept badly.
In the next-door room, Bulging
Brian snorted like a tethered bull and
every time he turned in his sleep the
floorboards shook. But it wasn't the
snoring or the shaking floorboards that
kept Clever Trevor awake. It was the
sound of a dog yapping and howling. It

was a strange, hollow sound. Sometimes it seemed to be coming from far away and sometimes it sounded as if it was coming from the hall.

Three times Clever Trevor went downstairs, and each time the yapping stopped when he reached the bottom step. Worst of all, every time he went back to his room, rain was pouring on to his bed because the window had mysteriously blown open.

After the third time, his bed was as wet as a sponge and he went to sleep in an armchair.

"Best sleep I've had for ages," said Bulging Brian the next morning, rubbing his eyes and yawning like a hippopotamus. He slapped thick slices of margarine on his bread, smeared lumps of peanut butter over the top and covered the lot in a snowstorm of sugar.

"Didn't you hear that dog yapping?" asked Clever Trevor. He was standing in the doorway in a filthy temper. His brand new white trainers were covered in mud and he had ripped his shiny yellow track suit on a rusty nail.

"Dog?" said Bulging Brian. "What dog? I didn't think there was a dog here."

"Nor did I," muttered Clever Trevor as he pulled bits of straw out of his hair and dropped them on the floor.

"Why are you wearing straw in your hair?" asked Bulging Brian through a mouthful of sugar and peanut butter.

"I'm not wearing straw," muttered Clever Trevor. "I was in the barn giving the cows their corn." He paused and looked superior. "You wouldn't understand."

As he spoke he remembered the surprised look on the cows' faces as he had scattered the corn on the ground. They hadn't seemed to understand either.

"Gosh," said Bulging Brian, looking impressed. He slurped his tea like a camel at a water trough. "What about the sheep?"

"Oh, they're scratching for worms and building nests right now," said Clever Trevor in a knowing way. "It's better not to disturb them."

Bulging Brian looked puzzled. "That's funny," he said. "I've got a picture book that says—"

Clever Trevor glared at him. "I don't need a picture book to tell me how to run my farm," he snapped, pouring tea into one of Great Aunt Emily's china cups. Then through the kitchen door, he caught sight of the portrait. The stream of tea overflowed into the saucer, ran over the table and poured on to the floor.

Great Aunt Emily's face had changed.
Snapper's face had changed.
Great Aunt Emily was scowling.
Snapper was showing his teeth and
looked as if he was growling.

Bulging Brian stood up and pulled
on his black and yellow leather biking
jacket. Then he wiped his mouth with
a tea towel. "Better get back and startle
a few swimmers," he said, sticking out
his chest and flexing his muscles. "Now

you're a farmer, you don't have to worry about all that."

"You're right," said Clever Trevor, still staring at the painting. "I don't have to worry about anything, anymore."

As he spoke, an idea occurred to him and a completely different look crossed his face. It was a worrying sight. Bulging Brian was about to ask if he'd hurt himself when Clever Trevor said, "Will you help me move that painting? I want to put it somewhere else. Like on top of the rubbish dump."

Bulging Brian looked at the portrait of Great Aunt Emily. "Do you think you ought to?" he asked slowly. "I mean, it was her farm after all."

Clever Trevor stuck out his lower lip and thrust his square jaw into the air. He looked tougher than ever before. "It's my farm now," he said. "I can do what I like."

Bulging Brian thought about this. Something still didn't seem right but he wasn't sure what. "Yeah," he said finally.

So Bulging Brian lifted and pulled and Clever Trevor gasped and tugged. Nothing happened. The painting of Great Aunt Emily wouldn't budge.

It was as if it was fixed to the wall with concrete.

changed. It was purple.

Then Clever Trevor noticed something
that made his mouth drop open and his
knees knock. Snapper had disappeared

from the painting!

Clever Trevor didn't stop to comb his
hair or change his clothes. He jumped
straight into the buttercup-yellow sports

"Tell you what," said Bulging Brian as he climbed on to his motorbike. "Why don't you get someone to come and paint over the top of it? The other day, I saw a man drawing terrific pictures on the pavement outside the swimming pool."

Clever Trevor remembered the pictures. They were full of palm trees, golden beaches, turquoise seas and girls in bikinis wearing lipstick. "That's a good idea," he said. "Send him out tomorrow." He walked back to the house as Bulging Brian roared out of the yard like a two-ton bumblebee. Inside, the colour of Great Aunt Emily's face seemed to have

car.

"You're working too hard," he told himself, as the car bounced down the muddy track. "You need a break."

Five minutes later, as he walked through the door of the *Skipping Pig Inn*, Clever Trevor had convinced himself that he had imagined everything.

Chapter Four

Henry and Hilda Bucket had owned *The Skipping Pig* for many years. They had known Great Aunt Emily well and it was their only daughter Nellie who had been helping out at Molehills Farm.

At first they were pleased to see Clever Trevor.

"You sit yourself down," said Hilda Bucket, who was large and friendly and made an elephant seem like a cuddly toy. "What would you like?"

"Tomato juice and lemonade," said Trevor, as he pulled a chair in front of the fire and hogged all the heat.

"It's hard work being a farmer," said Henry Bucket from behind the bar. "You're sure you want a cherry in your, um—"

"Cocktail," said Clever Trevor rudely. "I only drink cocktails." He paused. "And I want two cherries and an umbrella."

Henry Bucket stared at him and his big red nose began to glow with anger. "We...don't...have...umbrellas," he said slowly.

Clever Trevor frowned. "Then make it three cherries, a straw and a sugar cube," he said sulkily.

"Coming up," said Henry Bucket in an icy voice.

Clever Trevor spent the whole day at *The Skipping Pig*. He talked about his days as a lifeguard, how important he was, the height of his high chair and what hard work it had all been. Not once did he mention his Great Aunt Emily or Molehills Farm.

"How is the farm?" said Hilda Bucket at last, hoping that Clever Trevor would take the hint and go back to look after his animals. "Your aunt was very proud of her farm. She looked after it all by herself."

"Did she?" said Clever Trevor sounding bored.

"Of course, Snapper was a great help," continued Hilda Bucket. "He was always with her."

"Was he?" said Clever Trevor yawning.

Hilda Bucket looked at her watch. It was past seven o'clock and she knew the cows would need milking.

"How are the cows?" she asked pointedly. "They're a prize-winning herd, you know."

"That right?" said Clever Trevor, staring moodily into his empty glass. "Well, they may have won prizes but they haven't laid a single egg since I've been there. And I like an egg for my breakfast."

Henry and Hilda looked at each other with open mouths. They couldn't believe what they had just heard.

"Nellie's been up to help of course,"
said Hilda Bucket grimly.

Clever Trevor looked up. "You mean
that funny-looking girl with the bobble-
hat and glasses?" He leaned forward.
"The one that doesn't even wear
lipstick?"

"Sounds like my daughter," said Henry
Bucket in a low, furious voice.

But Clever Trevor wasn't listening.
"She tried to tell me about farming," he
sneered. "As if I didn't know anything."

Henry Bucket glared at him. "It seems to me…" he said in a dangerous tone of voice. But he never finished his sentence because the door suddenly blew open and the sound of yapping filled the room. It was a strange, hollow sound and Clever Trevor had heard it the night before. The hairs on the back of his thick neck prickled horribly. Slowly, all the things he thought he had imagined at Molehills Farm crept back into his mind.

BAA! BAA! A flock of sheep thundered through the door! Tables and chairs went flying. Glasses and plates crashed to the floor.

Henry Bucket glared at Clever Trevor.

"These are your sheep!" he roared.
He was so furious, his big red nose
was flashing on and off like a beacon.
"They're hungry! Get out of here and
look after them!"

And before Clever Trevor knew what
was happening, Hilda Bucket had
thrown him into the dark, wet night and
driven the sheep out after him.

Chapter Five

Poor Clever Trevor! There he was, pushed on every side by a flock of hungry sheep, with no idea how to get them back to Molehills Farm.

Suddenly, there was a sharp pain in his ankle. Then another and another. Something was biting him! Something with sharp teeth and a cold wet nose!

Clever Trevor looked down, but all he could see were sheep. Then he heard the sound of a dog growling, the same strange, hollow growling he had heard in the sitting room at Molehills Farm and now he knew which dog it was! It was the dog that had disappeared from the painting of his Great Aunt Emily. It was Snapper!

The butterflies in Clever Trevor's stomach grew propellers. Knees knocking, he leapt over the top of the sheep, jumped into the buttercup-yellow car and roared down the muddy track.

The painting was waiting for him when he pushed open the front door. Great Aunt Emily was still there, but now the long, knobbly stick was raised above her head as if she was going to hit somebody with it.

Clever Trevor couldn't help himself. He ducked and ran into the sitting room.

All the windows were open and the room was full of chickens!

Clever Trevor put his hands over his face and threw himself down on a chair.

Squelch! Squelch! Squelch!

He jumped up. A dozen broken eggs lay in a sticky yellow mess on the seat of the chair.

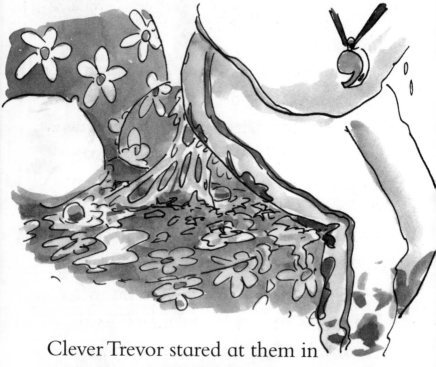

Clever Trevor stared at them in amazement. Chickens? Eggs?

Slowly his mind began to turn things over.

Then another even more extraordinary thought came to him. That must mean that cows not chickens had to be milked. And…Clever Trevor groaned aloud. Maybe sheep didn't scratch for worms after all. He thought of Henry Bucket's angry words: "These are your sheep! They're hungry!" Maybe he was right. Maybe the sheep really were hungry.

For the first time in his life, Clever Trevor felt completely unsure of himself. Maybe he didn't know as much about farming as he thought he did. No wonder Nellie Bucket had given him such a strange look. Perhaps he should borrow Bulging Brian's picture book after all.

A cold, nasty feeling crawled across Clever Trevor's stomach. He began to feel as if he had made a complete fool of himself. It was a brand new feeling, and he didn't like it one little bit.

Grrrr! Grrrr! Clever Trevor spun round and found himself staring straight into the fierce brown eyes of the terrier in the painting.

Clever Trevor tried to push him away with his foot, but his foot went straight through him and out the other side! Before Clever Trevor had time to faint, the terrier grabbed hold of his shiny yellow track suit and dragged him out of the room and down the hall to Great Aunt Emily. Clever Trevor didn't want to look up at her but soon felt the nip of Snapper's sharp teeth in his ankle. He looked up.

Great Aunt Emily's eyes were blazing and her arm was raised with her finger pointing to the yard!

Clever Trevor opened the door and Snapper tugged him across the muddy yard until they came to the rosebush on the other side.

Lying in the mud was the battered dog bowl he had thrown out of the window the day before. It seemed like a lifetime ago.

Clever Trevor bent down and picked it up, then with Snapper growling at his heels he walked back into the house, down the hall, into the sitting room, and put the dog bowl back on the wall above the fireplace.

Brrrrm! Brrrrm!

Bulging Brian's tyres squealed in the yard and for a second Trevor's white face was caught in the headlight of the motorbike. He looked down at his feet. Snapper had disappeared!

Clever Trevor ran into the hall just as Bulging Brian strode in to the house holding a picture book in his hand. Behind him was Nellie Bucket, carrying a box of groceries. This time she didn't give Trevor a strange look. Instead she looked as if she was sorry for him.

"It's hard work being a farmer," said Nellie Bucket kindly. "I brought you these in case you haven't had time to make supper."

"Yeah," said Bulging Brian. "And I brought you my picture book." For a moment, he looked embarrassed. "You can keep it," he added in a gruff voice.

Clever Trevor stared at them both. At first he couldn't think of anything to say.

"Thank you," he mumbled at last, blushing from head to toe. "I don't think I've been very clever." He took a deep breath. "In fact, my real name is Trevor Prat and I think I've been a right one for a long time."

Nellie Bucket grinned at him. "I'll milk the cows. You give the chickens their corn and Brian will feed the sheep," she said. She paused and there was a twinkle in her eye. "Then we'll have supper."

As she spoke, Clever Trevor looked up at the painting of Great Aunt Emily. In one hand she held Snapper and her other hand rested on a long, knobbly stick. The painting was exactly the same as when he had first arrived, except maybe, just maybe, there was a tiny smile on Great Aunt Emily's fierce, bristly face.